A Poisonous Mind

Ned Fain, Private Investigator, Book 5

A Hard-boiled Mystery

Sam Abbott

Sam Abbott

A Poisonous Mind: Ned Fain, Private Investigator, Book 5
Copyright © 2015 Liz Dodwell
www.mix-booksonline.com

Print ISBN-10: 193986027X
Print ISBN-13: 978-1-939860-27-9

Published by Mix Books, LLC

Table of Contents

One

If there is one thing I know about women, it's that I know almost nothing about women. That should be the motto and byword of every male of the human species, but it often amazes me how many men think they've got the other side all figured out. Me? I'm not one of those. I know nothing about how their minds work, and I've come to the conclusion that if I did know, it would probably scare me to death and ruin any hope of happiness I might have. I'll stay in the dark, thank you very much.

The thing that was prompting me down this road of reverie on that particular morning was the cup of coffee that Sylvi brought me when she came to work and woke me up.

Sylvi's my secretary and assistant. She handles the office and such, and sometimes works with me on jobs I take.

I'm Ned Fain, Private Eye. It says so on my front window, and I live in the back room of my office because it costs a lot less than having a separate apartment. I've got a bathroom, a small kitchenette, a huge sofa and a wide screen TV; what else can a bachelor want?

Sylvi comes in most mornings before I bother to get up, and brings me coffee and donuts. She usually wakes me up, unless she's mad at me; then I find the coffee on the side table, or if she's really ticked, out front on my desk.

On this particular morning, she must not have been too mad at me, because she came in and set it down on the side table, and woke me up as she was going back out front.

I reached for it, and that's when I saw the magazine article she'd carefully set it down on.

Romance In The Workplace: How To Work Together When You're In Love With Your Boss.

I better back up. Sylvi is twenty two, I'm thirty six. Sylvi is beautiful, I'm ugly as sin from some scars that I got in the Middle East. Sylvi is, in so many ways, the most wonderful woman that I've ever known; I'm an old grouch who pretty much hates the world and almost everything in it. And somehow, I'm in love with Sylvi. I've worked hard to keep my feelings from showing, but I guess I didn't do too good a job.

A couple weeks ago, I was on a case that got completely out of control, and ended up with me wrecking my car and nearly dying. I was in a coma for several days, and when I woke up, Sylvi was there. I knew she cared about me, and in some ways I thought she was the best friend I'd ever had, so I wasn't all that surprised that she stayed and took care of me until the doctors let me go home, then drove me back to my place. When I was getting ready to go to bed that night, though, she didn't leave like always before. She shoved me over and told me that she knew I was in love with her, and that she was in love with me, too. We didn't make love, only held each other through the night, and in the morning it was like it never happened.

That is the only time the subject of our feelings had ever come up, so finding that article sitting under my coffee cup was a bit of a surprise. As I said, I know *nothing* about women.

I dragged my carcass off the couch, showered and got dressed, then carried coffee and article out front to sit down at my desk, and started reading through it.

One of the most difficult relationships to maintain without stress is the workplace relationship, and this is especially true when one side is subordinate to the other. The natural tendency toward power struggle in humans means that, while we may accept such roles on the job, those roles may not be able to filter over into the relationship itself, and this is probably good.

The article seemed to be saying that if you fall in love with your boss, it's hard to switch over to different roles after work. Like, if Sylvi were my boss on a job, and I wanted to be "the man" at home, I might have problems getting her to see things my way.

Personally, I didn't see a problem. I was undoubtedly the boss, but Sylvi did what I told her to do only when it suited her to do so; and besides that, it almost always turned out that what she did was what I *would* have told her to do if I'd had a brain in my head, so it was okay. I was pretty sure it would go the same way in a personal relationship, if we had one.

I tossed the magazine down on my desk and looked over at Sylvi. She had her back to me, which might mean I was in trouble, but I couldn't think of anything I'd done just lately that might have made her mad. She didn't look all tensed up, so that was another good sign. I cleared my throat, and she turned in her chair to smile at me, the best sign of all.

"Oh, hi, Ned," she said with that big, bright smile I love so much. "I didn't hear you come in."

"Sylvi," I said, "I'm deaf, not stupid." I flipped the magazine at her. "Wanna enlighten me?"

She sat there for a moment, and I could tell she was thinking of playing innocent and pretending she didn't know what I meant. I could see that she thought better of it, too.

She sighed. "Ned, we've been avoiding the subject for almost two weeks. We both know we're in love with each other, but we pretend nothing has changed. You jump and turn red if I catch you looking at me. When I try to be a little flirtatious, you frown at me. You have not *once* even asked me out since we talked about it. Do I have to be the one to take the first steps, here?"

I looked into her eyes, and thought for a long minute.

"Sylvi,"I said slowly, "I'm damaged goods. No matter how much you might like me, and maybe even you really do love me, there are parts of me that will never be right, not anymore. I can't put you in a position to have to deal with those things."

She tilted her head and glared at me. "PTSD? Think I don't know that? I've seen you duck and cover when a car backfires outside, and after what you've been through, I'm pretty sure that is a perfectly normal reaction. Or are you talking about your scars? Do you think I give a flying monkey's butt what you look like to anyone else? I know what I see, and it really isn't all that bad, so don't judge me by what you *think* I see; let me show you what I see, instead."

I didn't know how to respond to that, and I got nervous when she suddenly stood up and started walking slowly to me, coming around the side of my desk rather than sitting in the chair opposite mine, like usual. She had a look on her face that said she was going to make some kind of effort to get this resolved right then and there, and I felt myself getting ready to relax to the inevitable when the door opened.

Sylvi spun around with a big smile, and started toward the tall black man who entered. He had a dog with him, a big, fawn colored Belgian Malinois if I was correct, and the first thing I noticed was that both of them were limping. The man looked to be in his mid-thirties, like me. I didn't even want to guess about the dog.

"Hi," Sylvi said, "and how can we help you today?" She bent down and looked at the dog, who seemed to think she was every bit as gorgeous as I did, because he was instantly trying to nuzzle up against her. She giggled and petted him, looking up at his owner. "I hope this is okay, I just couldn't resist," she said.

The man smiled. "Ol' Alfie'll eat that up," he said loudly. "He loves the ladies, he does."

She stood up and led him over to my desk, and he sat down. Alfie took a position next to him and sat, as well.

I rose and leaned over the desk to shake his hand. "Ned Fain," I said.

"Jay Mosley," he replied, and his grip was strong and confident. He was still speaking loudly, and I figured he might have some hearing issues, like me. "I been hearing

9

some good things about you, Ned, and I hear tell you was an Army man. That right?"

I smiled and nodded. "I was," I said. "I was a JAG Officer, Army lawyer, in Afghanistan, that's where I got my beauty treatments. Grenade."

Jay nodded. "Me and Alfie, too. We were EOD, explosive ordnance detail. We were clearing a building full of ISIS when the bomb we were looking for went off. I was pinned under rubble, and my left leg was crushed; Alfie was hit by falling debris and had severe fractures to his pelvis and right hip, and we were the lucky ones. The rest of the squad didn't make it out."

"Sorry to hear that," I said.

"ISIS was all around, and one of 'em came through what was left of the building to make sure we was all dead. He found me and was about to put a bullet in my head, but Alfie used his one good back leg to jump and take the bastard down, and I managed to get my hands on his gun. That ended the problem, and we got dusted off a few hours later." "Dusted off" meant they were carried out by med-evac helicopter, I knew. "I lost my leg, but they patched Alfie up best they could, and gave us both honorable discharges. I adopted him under some new program—they used to just put Military War Dogs down when they were done with them, calling them 'obsolete equipment,' you believe that? Alfie ain't a piece of equipment, he's my partner and my friend."

I looked at the dog, and the thought that he might have been killed just because he'd been wounded or wasn't needed anymore made me angry. "I can believe it," I said, "but I'm glad they gave you the chance to keep Alfie with you." Alfie wagged his tail when he heard his name, and I looked back at Jay. "So, what can I do for you and Alfie, today?"

He reached into a pocket and took out a piece of paper, unfolded it and passed it to me. At first I thought it was a ransom note, because it was made of letters cut out of magazines, but it wasn't. It said:

Your wife is a whore and she was cheating on you with your best friend while you were in the war. She is still going to see him behind your back.

I read it through and looked up at Jay. "Do you believe this?" I asked him.

"Hell, no," he said. "I ain't even told my wife I got it. Jeez, man, my best friend is Henry Ochoa, and he runs *SAV*; that's the charity I work at, down on Monroe Street, Service Animals for Veterans, but we call it SAVE cause it's easier to remember."

I smiled. "What does SAVE do?"

"Henry goes and rescues dogs from shelters, where they might get put down, then trains them to be guide dogs, mobility dogs, hearing dogs and such for disabled vets. We work with the Wounded Warrior Project, too. Me and Alfie help out with training some of them."

Sylvi was listening, and she came over then to sit on the floor next to Alfie, who didn't need a lot of prompting to lay down and let her rub his belly. I watched, hoping to pick up some pointers. She'd never rubbed my belly, and we were supposed to be trying to find a way to have a relationship…

I stopped that line of thought quickly.

Jay was still talking. "I haven't had a chance to get a real, paying job since I got home last year, but I get a pension. It's not much, but I'll pay you what I can, if you'll see if you can find out who's behind this…"

Sylvi butted in.

"Jay, don't worry about it," she said, "Ned does Pro Bono work sometimes, and he's short on it for this quarter. No charge."

That was probably the smoothest lie I'd ever seen her tell. I don't do pro bono work unless I get stiffed on payment, but the look of relief on Jay's face made me so proud of that girl at that moment that if I wasn't already in love with her, I'd be falling fast.

"Okay, good, that's settled," I said with a smile of my own. "So, if I get this right, this Henry is the best friend your wife is being accused of cheating with."

"Right. And ain't no way I believe it, from either of 'em."

"Then the place to start would probably be with him. I'll need to tell him about the note and what it says, is that all right with you?"

He nodded. "That's fine. I'll tell him you'll be stoppin' by." He started to get up and leave.

"OK," I said, "but don't tell him why. I want to see his face when I tell him about the note and the accusation. I'm sure it's not true, but there may be other information to be learned by watching body language."

Jay nodded. "No problem, I won't say why. Just a guy named Ned'll be stoppin' by, right?"

"Perfect. If you'll give Sylvi your contact information, I'll be in touch as soon as I have anything to report."

"Man," he said, "I can't thank you enough. This is hard when you ain't got no one to talk to, Ned, I surely thank you."

Once more I said, "No problem," and Jay made his way out the door with Alfie by his side, looking up at him lovingly. Sylvi and I watched as they got into a small car and drove away.

I turned to Sylvi and was about to bring up our earlier conversation, but the doggone door opened again, and a lady walked in at that moment. I knew instantly that she must be Jay's wife, because she was also black, like him, and was watching carefully to be sure that Jay and Alfie were out of sight as she shut the door behind herself. As soon as she was certain she hadn't been seen coming in, she turned to look at me and Sylvi.

"I hope you'll forgive me for doing this, and understand," she said. "I'm Gwen Mosley. That was my husband who just left here, and I—please, I need to know what he wanted."

"Ma'am, I'm sorry, but I can't tell you that. I'm bound by client confidentiality, just like an attorney."

She started to cry, and Sylvi quickly went to her and got her sitting down across from me.

"You've got to understand," she said, "that it's been a long road to recovery for Jay, and for Alfie, too. In fact, the dog is doing better than he is. Jay's still got quite a ways to go, especially in the, you know, emotional side of things. He's still having nightmares, and that prosthetic leg — he can use it to get around, but I see him sometimes, he sits and cries while he's putting it on."

"I can imagine that's rough," I said, not mentioning my own bouts with PTSD. "Unfortunately, I still..."

"Jay hasn't had it easy since he got back. He doesn't really want to be a civilian, and now that he's not on duty anymore, he's not having it easy being a full time husband, either. He feels like he's not accomplishing anything, like without that leg, he's not a whole man, anymore. He hasn't been able to get a job; he works at volunteer things to keep busy, and I'm doing all I can to help him, you know?" She blushed a bit, and looked down at her hands. "He's trying, though, and — he doesn't know yet, but we're pregnant."

Sylvi lit up like a Christmas tree. "Oh, Gwen, that's wonderful! That should help him, don't you think? Being a Daddy?"

Mrs. Mosley smiled, but sadly. "I haven't told him yet," she said. "He's been so — withdrawn, so cold, sometimes. I saw where he jotted down a note about coming to see you this morning, so I took some time off work and followed him, to try to find out what's going on." She suddenly began to sob, and Sylvi slid her chair closer to put an arm around the woman's shoulders. "I'm just scared

14

something must be terribly wrong, and I don't know what to do."

I frowned. "Mrs. Mosley, I do understand," I said, "but I honestly can't tell you anything I spoke to your husband about."

Sylvi turned to look at me, and glared, then turned back to Mrs. M.

"Ned can't, but I can. He came here because someone sent him a letter that says you were cheating on him with his best friend, Henry, while he was on overseas duty. He doesn't believe it, and he wants Ned to find out who's doing it."

I was about to tell Sylvi to shut up, when Mrs. Mosley suddenly looked shocked.

"A letter? One made up out of cut up letters from magazines? I got one, too, the other day, but I threw it away 'cause I didn't want Jay to see it. It said he was doing terrible things in Iraq, said he killed babies and fed them to Alfie, horrible things!"

I leaned forward. "Is there any chance you can find it again?" I asked her, but she shook her head.

"No, I'm sorry, I burned it up with the trash. I didn't want to take any chance Jay might see it. And let me tell you something else, there isn't any truth at all in that about me and Henry! Neither one of us would do such a thing, and especially not to Jay!"

I sat there for a moment, then told her that I thought she should go home and talk to her husband, tell him about the letter she'd gotten, and that she already told me about it.

Sylvi encouraged her when she started to stall, and by the time she left, she was smiling and planning to go to tell him everything.

I sat there for a minute, debating on whether to try to go back to the conversation I was having with Sylvi before Jay appeared, or to tell her just how ticked I was that she violated client confidence. I finally decided not to do either one.

"Go over that letter," I said, "and see if you can figure out anything that'll help, while I go see Henry Ochoa." I got up and stalked out the door without another word, and the look on her face told me that she knew I was unhappy with her.

Two

When I'd wrecked my car a couple weeks before, I'd been working on trying to prove that people were dying in strange ways after playing cards at a certain club. I'd been drawn into the case by a woman who claimed to be a reporter trying to get a story, and it turned out that she knew more than she was letting on.

Anyway, when I exposed the fact that the deaths had nothing to do with the club, the owner decided to give me a nice reward, or I should say, a couple of nice rewards. One of them was a nice, healthy check, which I desperately needed. The other was a 1969 Ford Mustang Cobra Jet, with 428 super power engine and four speed tranny, and more horsepower than just about anything on the road for its time. As I left Sylvi sitting there thinking about why I was mad, I walked down the alley to the garage I rent to keep the car in, got into that dream machine and backed it out into the street.

There's something about driving a true, original muscle car that makes all the modern super cars seem weaker than they are. The way the big engine chugs down when you're shifting, then roars back to life when you power into the throttle. Or the sense of control you get when you downshift and drift the car through a hard, right angle turn — that's driving, man, that's *driving*!

I went to the address Jay had given me for SAVE, and found it with no problem. I walked inside and a lady asked me how she could help me.

"I'm here to see Mr. Ochoa, if he's in. I'm a friend of Jay Mosley."

She looked me over briefly and came to exactly the conclusion I thought she would. "Oh, you must be looking for a service dog, right? Come on in, I'll tell Henry you're here."

When a man with burn scars all over his face, and a serious limp 'cause half his foot's missing, walks into a place that provides services to wounded vets, it's a pretty safe bet he's gonna be mistaken for a client. I let it slide, since it probably got me in to see Henry faster than telling the truth would have done. A moment later, the lady came back and ushered me into a back office.

A big man was in the chair behind the desk, and he stood when I entered. The lady closed the door behind me, and Henry Ochoa stuck out a hand. I shook it.

"You're looking for a service dog, Mr…"

"Fain, Ned Fain," I said, "and no, I'm not. I'm actually here at the request of Jay Mosley, who I'm told is a good friend of yours?"

Ochoa narrowed his eyes, but didn't look upset. "Yeah, my best friend, actually. What can I do for you, Mr. Fain?" He motioned for me to have a seat, and then returned to sit in his own chair.

"Mr. Ochoa…"

"Nope, Henry."

I smiled. "Henry, I'm a private detective. Jay came to see me today because he's gotten what I'd call a 'poison pen' letter. Someone sent him a letter made like a ransom note, with cut out letters and words, telling him that you and Jay's wife have been carrying on an affair while he was overseas."

Henry didn't jump to his feet, as I'd expected him to do. Instead, he cocked his head to one side and said, "Did they, now?" He sat forward and reached into a desk drawer, then pulled out a sheet of paper and passed it to me. It was just like the one Jay got, but it accused Henry of stealing money from SAVE.

"This appeared on my desk a few days back," he said.

I looked up at him. "Who has access to your office?"

He shrugged his shoulders and made a sheepish smile. "Pretty much anyone, I guess. I never lock it, it's always open. The only ones here all the time are myself and Leigh, my assistant, and Zandra, our secretary. She wasn't here the day I got it, though, had to take some time off for a family thing."

I nodded, because I'd expected as much. "So, is there any money missing?"

"Hang on a second," he said, then yelled out, "Leigh? Come in here!" A moment later, a fairly tall woman came in. Her bearing said she was ex-military, and I recognized it instantly. Henry smiled at her and then turned back to me.

"This is Leigh Cullen, my assistant director, and all around invaluable asset." he said.

I smiled. "I've got one of those. Mine forgets who the boss is a lot, does yours?"

The rudeness of my question would be obvious to most people, but Henry and Leigh only smiled at each other. I'd learned what I wanted to know; these two had a very

19

close personal relationship, as well as an obviously effective working one.

"She tends to tell me what to do, I guess, but she's usually right so I let her get away with it. Yours like that?"

"Yeah, pretty much." We chuckled together while Leigh glared at him, but there was a smile lurking underneath it, I could tell. Henry turned to her.

"When I got that letter," he said, "I called Leigh in and we went through the books with a fine tooth comb. There is absolutely nothing out of order in the accounts, and I'd be glad to open them for auditing at any time."

Leigh piped up. "I got one of those, too, the same day as Henry. Let me go get it." She stepped out and was gone for only a few moments, then came back and handed me another letter. This one said that Leigh was "a domineering, asexual bitch" and "verbally abusive to SAVE's clientele."

"Somebody is not your fan," I said to Leigh, and Henry snorted.

"Yeah, well, the worst part of it is that it's absolutely not true. Everybody who comes to us loves her to pieces, from the people to the dogs themselves. She knows what it's like to come back from over there, face life back here after the things we all saw and had to do."

Leigh nodded. "I drove a Humvee in Baghdad; there was a lot of things went down over there that I wish I didn't remember, and while I might not be as bad off as some, I have my share of nightmares. I feel for these people who come in here, and I'd never talk down to them."

I believed her. Like both of these people, I knew the pain of PTSD, knew what it felt like to wake up thinking you're back in the situation that almost killed you. They'd never abuse anyone, and the work they did was obviously their mission in life. I didn't believe they'd abuse the trust that so many people placed in them.

"Okay," I said, "that's all I need for now. Do me a favor, though," I said. "Ask around, quietly, see if anyone else connected with SAVE has gotten one of these, and let me know. This isn't about things that happened overseas. I'm thinking it's about something connected to all of you."

They agreed, and then Leigh made me copies of their letters. I headed back to the office, but since it was almost noon, I called ahead and Sylvi answered.

"Ned Fain, Private Eye," she said, and I snickered like I did every time I heard her answer the office phone that way.

"Sylvi, it's me," I said. "You hungry? Wanna go out for lunch?"

She was quiet for a minute, then, "You still mad at me for talking too much?"

"Nah. I can't stay mad at you," I said, and then I took a deep breath. "I love you too much for that."

There was dead silence on the phone for a good thirty seconds, and I was about to decide I'd blown it for good, when she said, "I love you, too. So where are you taking me for lunch?"

I smiled, and I think I almost split my face. "Let's go to the Rialto. I'm feeling like having a steak, and maybe we can get one of those romantic little booths with the candles."

"*Ooh*," she said, "romantic, huh? Does this mean you're gonna stop being afraid to talk about us?"

"It means I'm hungry, I want a steak and I want to look at the most beautiful girl in the world while I eat it. Take what you can get, Gorgeous."

She laughed delightedly. "I'll take it. How far out are you, do I have time to freshen up?"

"You got about ten minutes, and I'll be out front. Bye," I said, and cut the call off.

I was still smiling. Could it really be that a man who was as messed up as I was could find a beautiful girl who would look past the scars? Did I even deserve a girl like Sylvi? I decided to save all those questions for another day, preferably sometime in a hundred years or so, and just concentrated on getting to the office to pick her up.

When I pulled up, Sylvi came rushing out and jumped in before I could get out to open her door, then leaned across the console and kissed me right on the lips. "It's about time you started paying attention to me, Old Man," she said, and I laughed.

"No problem, Little Girl," I threw back, and then shoved the four speed into first and left a little rubber on the road in front of the office. She watched me shift through the gears, and then took my hand when I got it into high.

"Ned," she said, "what do you want? From this, I mean? Do you want me to be your girlfriend, do you want

22

to just take it slow? Tell me what you want, I don't want to push you into anything."

I glanced at her, then put my eyes back on the road, where they belonged. "Isn't that supposed to be my line?" I asked. "Shouldn't I be asking you that question?"

She squeezed my hand. "Then ask it," she said, "but don't get upset if you don't like my answer."

I looked at her again, a second longer this time. "Okay. What do you want from this, Sylvi? You're young and beautiful, and if we're together, you're going to have all kinds of people thinking you're after me for my money or something, because no one is gonna believe you might actually care about an old scarecrow like me. Y'know?"

She didn't say anything for a moment, but then she squeezed my hand again.

"I want to tell my mom that I'm dating my boss, the guy who saved my life," she said. "I want to tell her and other people that I'm in love with you, and I don't give a big fig what they think. I want to sit close to you in a restaurant, and hold your hand when we go places, and I want you to lean over and kiss me whenever you want to, like you did at the Granny Mae club, and make every man around get jealous and wonder what you've got that they don't. And I want *you* to know that what you've got that they don't... is *me*."

I swallowed hard, a big lump in my throat. "Sylvi—I want all of those things, too," I said, "but I don't want you to feel like I'm pressuring you for anything else, either. I know some guys..."

"Oh, don't worry," she said quickly, rolling her eyes a bit, "we're not going there, not yet, anyway. One thing you're gonna find hard to believe about me, especially since you know I danced my way through college, is that I still have my V-card, and I'm planning to keep it until I get married!"

I maneuvered the car through a turn, downshifting and then shifting back up to high, and then looked at her. "What is a V-card? Is that like a Veteran's Dependent card or something?"

She burst out laughing so hard that I was startled, and then I was laughing with her, but I didn't know why. She tried to speak about three times before she finally got herself under control.

"Oh, my gosh," she said, wiping tears of laughter away, "Ned—I'm telling you that I'm still a virgin! I made myself a promise in high school that I wouldn't give it up until I was married, so if you've got any plans in that direction, you better be thinking diamonds and gold! If there ain't no ring, Baby, then there ain't no fling!"

I think my face was red, and my eyes were wide. "I'm perfectly okay with that," I said, but a part of my subconscious was calling me a liar. I mean, I'm human, so if I said the thought of making love to her didn't cross my mind, I'd be one, for sure. On the other hand, there was something about the way she said it that made me proud of her, so I was more than willing to honor that commitment. Or was she saying she wanted me to propose?

Was I ready for that step? I'd been married once, but my wife hadn't been able to cope with what happened to me; one look at the new me, and she was my new ex-wife. Thank God we hadn't had any kids!

I looked at Sylvi as I turned into the Rialto parking lot. "So, are you saying you want me to think about diamonds?"

It was her turn to suddenly get wide eyes. "Well," she said, "not necessarily right away—but maybe, if things go the right direction, we could—discuss it."

I was out of the car and around to open her door before she got a chance to think. We went inside, and sure enough, Tomas, the Maitre D, was happy to give us one of the more private booths. We sat down and gave our drink orders—coffee for me, and a sweet tea for Sylvi—and made small talk as we waited for the waiter bring them.

When we'd placed our full order, I looked at Sylvi. "As much as I like thinking about us," I said, "I do have to work on this case for Jay Mosley, and it's taking some odd turns. I've found out that his friend Henry has also gotten one of those letters, and so did Henry's assistant, Leigh Cullen." I showed her the two copies, and she read through them. "Whoever is doing this is somehow connected to their organization."

Sylvi nodded. "Yeah, has to be. And it's someone who can get access to the office. Who all can?"

"According to Henry, only he and Leigh and their secretary have keys to the building, and the secretary wasn't there the day these showed up. It could be one of the volunteers, of course, possibly even Jay If he's warped

25

enough, he could be doing it and not even know it, consciously."

She shook her head. "No, I don't think it's him. He had too much pain in his face when he showed us the letter he got. I think if he'd done it, he'd have only shown us his anger. That's what he'd figure we'd expect to see, right?"

I shrugged. "You're probably right, but we can't rule him out completely. And we don't know how many other volunteers there are."

We talked about it all the way through lunch, and when we were done eating, we got up to head back to the office. As we stood, Sylvi slid out of the booth and I found myself close to her, so I reached out and took hold of her arm and pulled her over close to me—and kissed her.

It wasn't hard, or passionate. It was just a kiss, and I wanted it to say to her that I was glad she was with me, and that I cared for her, and nothing else. From the smile it got me, I think it said that fairly well.

When we got to the office, Sylvi saw the voicemail light on the phone and checked it, then told me to call Henry Ochoa. I dialed the number she wrote down for me and put it on speakerphone. It helps me hear what's being said better.

"SAVE," answered the secretary, "how can I help you?"

"Henry Ochoa, please," I said, and the woman didn't even ask why I was calling. Henry answered a moment later.

"Henry, it's Ned Fain," I said. "I got a message to call you?"

"Yeah, thanks, Ned. We found out about three more letters that all seemed to appear around the same time. The only one who kept it was Doctor Morgan, a semi-retired physician who works with SAVE to help out some of the vets, and it accuses him of dealing drugs, pushing painkillers and such, which is bogus. The others are Zandra, the secretary, she got one that said she was ugly and smells. And then there's one of our volunteer trainers, Deanna Spence; she got one that accused her of — well, some very despicable things with the dogs. If there are any others who got them, they're keeping quiet about it."

I thanked him and added the info to my notes, then turned to Sylvi.

"Whoever's doing this is out to ruin SAVE," I said, but she frowned.

"I've been thinking about the way they all seem to be attacking different people from different angles. It seems to me that poison pen letters are sort of, I dunno — maybe 'bitchy' would be the right word. A female-type thing, y'know?"

"Good point," I agreed. "They're not even logical; some of them just seem to be trying to insult the person who got it, and others actually accuse people of doing something, either illegal or at least immoral. The only thing they all have in common is that they're connected to SAVE."

"That means whoever's doing it is also connected, but we already figured that out. Most likely, all it really amounts to is somebody trying to start crap."

"Yeah, but things like this can cause a lot of damage to your reputation, your relationships—this is just the beginning, I'm sure."

"Well, I looked over the ones we've got, and I can tell you that they're all made up of letters cut from magazines and glued onto the same common glossy white copy paper. The ones that Jay and his wife got were mailed, and were sent from different post offices within the area, none of them from inside the city."

We kicked it around for the rest of the day, but nothing jumped out at us. I mentioned that there were stacks of magazines at the SAVE office, but I hadn't thought to look at them. We both agreed that the perp would be stupid to clip the letters right there, anyway.

We went out and grabbed a bucket of chicken for dinner, and then went into my room and kicked back on the couch. I sat on one end, and Sylvi sat close and leaned against me, and after a few minutes, I let my arm go around her and pull her closer. We sat there like that for a couple of hours, watching Sam and Dean chase shapeshifters and crossroads demons, and then Sylvi kissed me and made me forget all about Supernatural.

We let ourselves enjoy the feelings of being entwined in each other's embrace for a little while, and then we each pulled back at the same time. Sylvi kissed me goodnight and went home, and I actually turned off the TV and went to sleep, content for the first time in more than a year.

Three

I woke to Sylvi kissing my cheek, lightly and repeatedly, and pretended to stay asleep so she wouldn't stop too soon. When I sensed she was starting to worry about why I wasn't waking, I rolled over quickly and trapped her in my arms for a real kiss, then let her go. She smiled as she handed me my coffee, waggled the bag of donuts and sashayed her way back out front.

I got up and showered, then got dressed and carried my coffee out to the office. Sylvi was sitting on my desk, waiting for me. She fished me out a cinnamon glazed as I took my chair.

"Here," she said, and I smiled as she held it up to my mouth so I could take a bite.

"Thanks," I said while chewing, and she yanked it back before I could take another. "Hey!"

"No, no, no," she teased me. "The correct answer is, 'Thanks, *Baby*.' You have a girlfriend now, you've got to learn to treat her right!"

"Aha," I smiled. "Thank you, Baby! Thank you, Darlin'! Thank you, Honey! Am I catching on?"

"I can see you're gonna need a lot of practice, but we'll work on you. In a year or two, you'll have it all down pat." She pushed the donut to my mouth again, and I bit it right out of her hand, then chewed it up and swallowed it fast.

The phone rang as I took a big swig from my coffee, and Sylvi answered it on the extension on my desk.

"Ned Fain, Private..." Her eyes suddenly went wide, and she said, "Whoa, wait a minute, calm down! Who arrested him, and why?" She listened for a moment, then handed the phone to me, saying, "Henry Ochoa's been murdered, and the cops just arrested Jay Mosley for it."

I snatched the phone to my ear. "This is Ned, what's going on?"

Gwen Mosley was on the line, and she was sobbing. "Mr. Fain, I just had to call you. The cops just showed up here and said Henry's been killed, and they say they have a witness that puts Jay there when it happened. They came here to arrest him, and when they started slamming him around, Alfie growled at the cop who was doing it, and the other one shot him. Oh, Mr. Fain, I don't know what to do, please, please help us!"

I sent Sylvi to Jay's house with instructions to say I was representing Jay and his wife—I'm still a licensed attorney—and to tell Gwen to say absolutely nothing to them without me present, while I headed for the cop shop. Sylvi called me while I was on the way to tell me Gwen was in shock, that paramedics had been called by the cops, and insisted on taking her to the hospital when they found out she was pregnant.

"Good girl," I said. "Take care of her and don't let anyone bully her."

"I got this, Babe," she said.

Jay had been arrested by the suburban police where he lived, and where SAVE's offices were. I'd been there a few times on minor cases, and was known well enough to be disliked. I parked on the street in front of their PD and fed a few quarters into the meter, not sure how long I was going to be there. The desk sergeant looked up at me and groaned; he'd seen this mug one too many times not to know it meant trouble for someone when I came barging through the door.

"What do you need, Scarecrow?" he asked, using the nickname I'd gotten from a jackass detective named Carlson, back on my first case.

"Here to see my client, Jay Mosley," I answered.

The sergeant snickered. "Then come back Saturday, ten to two. Those are visiting hours."

I had been ready for this, and shoved my still-valid state Attorney ID Card in front of his eyes. "You just refused to allow a prisoner access to his attorney as required by both state and federal law. Want me to start the proceedings against you now, or do you think you can get past this stupidity and do something right?"

He looked at the card, and his brow wrinkled. "I thought you were a PI?"

"I'm also a licensed attorney, admitted to the Bar, and that is *my client* you've got back there being unlawfully questioned without my presence and advice. I'm gonna count to three — one — two..."

"Aw, geez, come on around!" He pressed a button and a door opened in the wall to my right that let me pass into the jail foyer. The jailer on duty, a woman, looked up as I came through.

"Mr. Fain," she said. "Who you here for?"

"Jay Mosley," I said, "I'm his attorney."

She scowled, but we'd been through this dance a couple times before, and she knew not to cross me. "Hang on a few minutes..."

"No," I said, "I won't. I want to see my client right now, or I'll be filing unlawful restraint charges on everyone in this building within fifteen minutes. He has the right to have me present before and during any questioning, and we both know he's back there right now under a hot spotlight with his rights being raped away. So unless you want your name on that list," I looked hard at her name tag, "Officer Ingles, you've got ten seconds to comply with my lawful demand for access to my client."

She was glaring at me by the time I finished, but she wasn't stupid enough to push me any further.

I was led to the room where Jay was being questioned, and was shocked by what I saw. Jay was handcuffed to a bench against the back wall, and four uniform officers were in the room with him. As I entered, one of them shoved Jay's head viciously back against the wall and shouted in his face, "Why'd you kill him, huh? Why'd you kill Henry? You gettin' jealous he's doing so well, and you're just a messed up bum? Was that it? Answer me, you son of a bitch!"

"Officer, have you advised my client of his rights?" I said firmly, and all four of them turned to look at me.

"What are you doing in here?" asked the mouthy one, and I flashed my ID again.

"I'm his attorney, and if you don't back off right now, I'm the son of a bitch who is going to cost you your career. My client has not been afforded a reasonable opportunity to consult with me before or during questioning, so you are in direct violation of his constitutional rights, and I would just love to ruin your life for that, but I'm gonna give you one chance to make it through this intact. *Now, get the hell out of here, all of you!"*

The jailer had followed me in, probably expecting to see me get shut down by the uniforms, but that didn't happen. Instead, she picked up a microphone on her shoulder and called for Jay to be brought to contact room one immediately.

A contact room is a visiting room where contact between prisoners and visitors is allowed. In some cases, a man may get a visit from his wife and children there, and they're allowed to share hugs and kisses. They're also used for attorney-client meetings, as long as the prisoner is not considered a danger to the attorney.

I was led into the room a moment after Jay, and we sat in chairs on opposite sides of a small table that was bolted to the floor. I took one look at him, and knew we had a problem. His eyes were darting all over the place, and every sound, even the scuff of my shoe on the floor, would make him flinch and duck. He was having flashbacks.

"Jay," I said softly, "it's Ned Fain. I'm here as your attorney, not your investigator. Remember that if anyone asks you, okay? I'm your attorney."

Jay nodded his head. "Roger that," he said. "Cap'n, I can't find Alfie. We gotta find Alfie."

Just great, he was in full blown traumatic shock. I patted his hand and said, "We'll find him, Jay. We'll find him."

I went to the door and knocked, and the jailer opened the communication window.

"Yeah?"

I smiled at her. "Hello, Dearie. My client is in shock and needs to be seen immediately by a doctor. I want him taken to the emergency room at Mercy Hospital, right now."

She looked at me for a moment, then said, "I'll have to see when I can get someone to..."

"Did I stutter? Did it sound for even one second that I was making a request? This man is in need of medical attention, and if you do not get him moved to the ER within the next five minutes, I promise you that within six months, he and his wife will be getting eighty percent of your take home pay for the rest of your life. Understood?"

She slammed the window, and the door opened less than twenty seconds later. One of the jail nurses came in and looked at Jay, then yelled for someone to help her get him ready to go to the hospital.

Jay put up quite a fight, and they finally had to sedate him to get him into the ambulance. I had to sign some paperwork, and then some detective named Merkel who was supposedly in charge of the investigation into Henry's murder wanted to see me, so I got delayed for a few more minutes.

I told Merkel about the poison pen letters, handed over the ones I had, then asked about the dog, Alfie. Merkel was delighted to tell me that he'd been the one to shoot the dog.

"Dang thing jumped at my officer while he was trying to subdue the suspect," he said. "I fired one time, blew that dog into the next room!"

"You killed him? You stupid jackass, that dog was a decorated war hero!"

Merkel shrugged. "Who cares, it was growling at a cop! That makes it a threat and I took out that threat! Don't know if it's dead yet or not, the animal control people were lookin' for it when I left there."

I shook my head in disgust and left, grabbing my phone as I did so. I called Mick Mulcahy, the detective I'd worked with on previous cases.

"Mick, it's Ned. I've got a situation, I could use your help." I laid it out for him, and though it was a part of the city that was out of his jurisdiction, he didn't like what he was hearing.

"Let me see what I can find out, Ned, and I'll call you back."

By the time I got parked at the hospital and made it inside, the doctor on duty had already realized that Jay was experiencing wartime reactive shock, reliving something that had happened in Iraq, and started the process of admitting him. I was allowed to stay with him as he slept, and I used the time to try to figure out what to do.

About thirty minutes after I got there, Sylvi showed up with Gwen, and nurses put her into the same room with her husband. Sylvi came to me and whispered, "Anything on Alfie? Gwen says he ran away after he was shot, and they called out the dogcatchers to go after him."

I shook my head. "I didn't even know for sure he was alive. I've got Mick trying to find out what happened to him."

She put a hand on my shoulder, then started rubbing my back. "God, I hope he's okay. I mean, Gwen said he ran, so he might not be hurt too badly, right?"

"He's a tough soldier," I said. "All we can do right now is pray."

A couple of cops came in and wanted to talk to Jay and Gwen, but I ran them out. Jay stirred right after they left, and woke a moment later. He seemed to be somewhat coherent, so I asked him and Gwen to tell me what had happened.

"Me and the wife talked things over last night," Jay said. "I told her about the letter, and she told me about hers, and we both knew it was all bogus. Then Gwen told me we're gonna have a baby, and, well, things got a lot better. We ended up making up, and we were still in bed this morning when cops come busting down our door, sayin' I killed Henry and they had a witness. I was gonna go peacefully, but one of the cops was tryin' to prove he was tough, I guess, cause he grabbed me by my neck and tried to put me on the floor. That's when Alfie—Alfie growled at him, warning him, and that plainclothes cop just pulled a gun and shot him." Tears were flowing before he finished.

Gwen took up the story, then. "Jay screamed, and then he just sat down and put his arms over his head. Alfie let out a yelp, and ran off out the back door, and that was the last we've seen of him. That cop called in the rabies people, and told them Alfie was a mad dog and needed to be put down as soon as they could find him, and nobody would listen to me at all." She stifled a sob. "I started screaming, and they were dragging Jay out by his arms and shoving him into a police car, and one of the cops grabbed onto me and started shoving me around, but I yelled I was pregnant and he backed off. I blacked out then, and when I came to, I was laying down and there were paramedics, telling me they were taking me to a hospital, but I made them let me call you first. I hope that was the right thing to do—I was just so scared."

Sylvi caressed her shoulder. "It was exactly the right thing to do," she said. "Ned won't let anything happen to Jay."

The doctor came by a few minutes later, and I got him to transfer Jay to the VA hospital back in the city. They have their problems, but they also know more about PTSD and how to treat it than anyone else, so he agreed. Gwen would be released, since she was only shook up over all that was happening, but I told Sylvi to stay with her as much as possible. I didn't want anyone, cops included, trying to waylay her for more information.

Jay caught my hand as they were getting ready to wheel him out, with two cops going along. "Mr. Fain, what happened to Henry? Is he really dead? And please, please find out about Alfie for me!"

I told him that all I knew was that Henry was supposedly found shot to death. As for finding out about Alfie, I assured him I would. He let go of my hand and said he was ready to go, but at that very moment, my phone rang, and I saw that it was Mick calling.

"Ned," I said.

"It's Mick," he told me, unnecessarily. "I found the dog. The bullet went through his shoulder, and he's been found and taken to animal control. That ass Merkel told them the dog was dangerous and attacked an officer, so they decided to go ahead and put him down..."

"Oh, jeez, no!" I yelled, but Mick wasn't done.

"Calm down! I got hold of their office manager and told him that dog is a war hero, and if anything happened to him I'd personally make all of their lives a living hell! They took him to an animal ER right then, Jefferson Veterinary Clinic on Montrose Way. I called over there a couple minutes ago; they said the bullet went clean through without hitting anything vital. They're taking him into surgery on my authorization, and they say he's going to be fine."

"I'm on the way," I said and rang off. I turned to Jay and Gwen. "Alfie's alive, and he's been taken to an animal hospital. The bullet didn't do any serious damage, and he's going to be all right."

Both of them began crying tears of happiness.

Four

I went to check on Alfie, and found him doing okay, but sleeping. It had taken minor surgery to clean and close the wound, and he'd be out cold for a day or so, so I didn't disturb him. I made sure the vet knew I'd see that the bill got paid, and went back to the office.

The day wasn't even half over yet, so I made calls and got more information. Henry had been shot at fairly close range, a single shot to the heart, and there had been no signs of any struggle, so that fit with the idea that he'd known his killer and wasn't afraid. The police report says that there was a witness who saw Jay go into Henry's office late the afternoon of the day before, and Henry's body was discovered the next morning by Leigh Cullen. The witness was identified as the secretary, Zandra Daymude.

I filed all this away, but I didn't believe Jay was really the killer. Something wasn't adding up on it, and I tried all afternoon to figure out what it was. I was still at it when Sylvi came in around six.

"Gwen's doing a little better," she said, "and I've assured her that we won't give up until we get the truth. She's staying with Jay at the hospital, and said she'll be ready to do anything she can to help."

I nodded. "She's been through enough for today. I've been trying to get an angle on this whole thing. I mean, who on earth would want Henry dead?"

Sylvi bit her bottom lip. "Ned — Jay said he and Gwen didn't talk until last night, and that would be after Henry was already dead. Do you think there's a chance he might have actually done it? Maybe he flipped out and started to believe that letter was true, got jealous and killed him while he was out of his mind?"

"Yeah, I've considered that could be a possibility, but it doesn't feel right. Just my gut, but it's done me right before, so I'm gonna go with it until I find proof the other way."

We went back to my room and ordered pizza, then sat on the couch and just cuddled until it came. I was seriously out of practice on having a girlfriend, but I guess some things are like riding a bike — it all seemed to be coming back to me, slowly.

When the pizza arrived, Sylvi went to get it and bring it back to the room, and we ate it with Sam and Dean on the tube. I kept hoping for some inspiration to hit me, something that would suddenly show me how all these puzzle pieces fit together, but nothing came. When ten o'clock hit, Sylvi got up and said she was going home, but then she stopped and looked at me.

"If we get together, are you gonna move in with me, or would you want me to move in here?"

I looked at her for a second, then looked around the room. "What? You'd want me to give up all this luxury to come live in your apartment?"

She twisted her lips to one side and thought about it. "You're right," she said. "Move over, I'm sleeping here tonight."

I stared at her. "Sylvi—do you think this is a good idea? I mean, we agreed we're not doing anything unless we get married, but I don't know if I'm strong enough to resist temptation if you're snuggled up against me all night."

She smiled. "I can, and I can also kick your butt. Move over."

I never win.

We woke the next morning and went out for breakfast to a little diner where Mick likes to eat, and sure enough, there he was. He waved us into the other side of his booth and motioned for the waitress to come bring us coffee.

"How's your guy doing?" he asked me.

"He's shook up, but the fact you saved his dog has given him some strength. I think he'll be okay, if I can prove he didn't kill his friend."

"That may be tough," Mick said. "Merkel said they have a witness who's pretty solid, and knows your guy well. She says he came in looking angry about four, just as she was getting ready to leave for the day, and said it sounded like they were yelling at each other as she closed the door behind her. If you can't find anything else, that's enough circumstantial to get a conviction on murder two, at least. Anger, an emotional killing? Manslaughter might be the best deal he can get."

"Could be," I said, "but I'm not giving up yet. A guy like Jay looks angry all the time; PTSD will do that to you. And he always talks kind of loud, so it might have sounded like yelling, I guess. Gut hunch says he didn't do it, and I'm going with that."

Mick shrugged. "Your case. Let me know if I can help."

We got back to the office around eight, and the phone was ringing as we walked in. it was Detective Merkel.

"You wanted to know when we go to question your boy," he said. "Well, we'll be at his hospital room in ten minutes."

"No," I said. "You'll be outside his hospital room in ten minutes, but you won't enter it or speak to my client until I arrive, which will take me about thirty minutes. Got that?" I hung up without waiting for a response.

"I gotta go," I told Sylvi. "They're about to question Jay."

I went to get the car and headed for the VA hospital. I was halfway hoping Merkel wouldn't wait, just so I could file on him, but he did. I went into Jay's room first, to tell him that he should look at me before answering any question. If I didn't shake my head, he could answer; if I did, he was to refuse under the fifth amendment.

Merkel came in and stood right over Jay.

"Mr Mosley," he said, but I stopped him.

"Move back. You're here to ask questions, not badger him. You can do that sitting in a chair, I don't want you pressuring him to answer the way you think he should."

Merkel glared at me, but took a chair and sat down. Two other cops, in uniform, stood at his sides. They weren't looking at Jay, particularly, so I didn't object.

"Mr. Mosley, can you tell us why you went to see Henry Ochoa night before last?"

Jay glanced at me and I didn't move. He looked at Merkel and said, "Because he's my best friend."

Merkel snorted. "Remind me not to count you as a friend. Do you kill all your buddies?"

"Inappropriate question, Merkel," I said, and he turned to glare at me again.

"That's 'Detective Merkel' to you."

"When I see you acting like a detective, I'll treat you like one," I said bluntly, and he chose to ignore it.

"Witnesses say you were arguing with him. What were you angry about?"

Jay didn't even look my way. His eyebrows went up and he said, "I wasn't angry about anything. I stopped in to ask if I could get a few more hours a week to work with the dogs. Keep me busy, keep my mind off things"

"But by the time you left, he was dead. Can you explain that in any way that won't lead me to believe you killed him?"

"He was fine when I left. I wasn't even there ten minutes—he said, sure, he could get me more hours, and he had three new dogs coming in the next day, so he was glad I was volunteering. I said thanks, and left, and he was talking on the phone to someone else when I walked out."

Merkel made a note. "Mr. Mosley, do you own a handgun? A forty caliber?"

Jay glanced at me, but didn't wait for me to give him a cue. He turned back to Merkel.

"No, I don't," he said.

Merkel snorted again. "Oh, come on," he said. "What military man doesn't have at least one gun around?"

"One with PTSD, you dumb ass. Just looking at a gun messes me up, and the sound of a gun can send me right into traumatic shock."

"Well, if you didn't kill him, who did?"

"How the hell should I know? Henry was always the last one to leave, and the doors were always open if he was there. Anybody coulda walked in after I left."

I interrupted. "Merkel, what about the gun? Any leads on it?"

He shook his head without facing me. "Not yet. All we got is it's a forty caliber, and probably a Glock." He looked up at Jay. "Let me tell you what I think. You got this letter," and he produced the one Jay had received, "so you were pretty pissed that he'd been boinkin' your old lady. You got out your non-existent gun and went down there to tell him to leave her alone. He said you were nuts, which you are, and then you shot him, and split. You went home to the missus, made a big thing about making up with her, and figured you were home free. You just didn't know that the secretary saw you go in and heard you yelling at him. Way I see it, we got you dead to rights."

Jay sat up and I thought for a moment he was going to lunge at Merkel, but he didn't.

"You jackass, I knew damn well he didn't do no such thing, and neither did my wife! I never once believed that crap, I just wanted to know who was doing it! That's why I hired an investigator!"

The questions went on, and after hearing the same ones over and over for an hour or more, I called a halt to them. Merkel objected, but I got the doctor in, who said Jay was under extreme stress, and couldn't take any more right then. Merkel left in a tizzy, and I told Jay I'd be back later.

I left the hospital and went to see what I could learn about the others who were connected to SAVE and had received letters. They were all scheduled to be at SAVE that day, so I went on down to their building. Leigh was there, and seemed pretty upset, which was understandable. I asked if she was going to keep the place running, and commented that it looked like someone had been tidying up. Even the old stack of magazines was gone.

"The committee that runs it has already asked me to take over as interim director, and I'll probably get offered the full time position. It just isn't the same without Henry, but this was his dream, so I'll do all I can to keep it going."

"That's all you can do, I guess. I need to ask you some questions, if you're up to it."

She lifted one shoulder in a half shrug. "Sure. Cops already asked me most of them, anyway, I'm sure."

"You were the one who found Henry, yesterday, right?"

She nodded, and I saw tears leaking down her cheeks. "Yeah. He was sitting right here at his desk, just slumped backwards. Whoever did it had to have been someone he knew, because they got really close. I've seen gunshot wounds many times, and this one was fired from no more than four or five feet away. On top of that, there was no sign of a fight or anything, and nothing was missing, so it wasn't a robbery. And no, I don't believe Jay killed him. Those two were close."

I waited a moment, then asked, "What about anyone else Henry might have had a problem with? I know you and he were close, too; is there an ex-husband that might have had a grudge against him?"

She laughed, but it was sarcastic. "Not hardly," she said. "My ex was so glad to get rid of me he paid for the divorce and gave me a new car in the deal. He never even met Henry, and probably doesn't even know where I live, now. We were in Florida two years ago when I caught him cheating on me, and we haven't been face to face since that night. And honestly, Henry didn't have enemies. I don't think anyone ever disliked him, he was one of the sweetest guys you'd ever have a chance to know." She grinned. "Hard to believe he was a Navy Seal, and one of the most dangerous guys on the planet."

That backed up the theory that the killer was someone Henry trusted; not too many people could get the drop on a Seal, unless he had no reason to suspect he was in danger.

"Okay," I said, "tell me about the people who got these letters, other than Gwen and Jay, and yourself, of course."

She thought about it for a moment. "Well, Doctor Morgan got one. He's about the best thing that's happened to us. He started out as a MASH surgeon in Viet Nam, a career army man, so he saw a lot of war wounded in his career. He helps out with the vets we work with, this is all he does now. He's retired, and the fact that he is also gay made it hard for him in the Army. He knows what it's like to be alone and have no one, so he thinks this is a great program."

"Okay."

"Zandra, our secretary, she's been with us about a year now. She's not a volunteer, she gets a paycheck, and to be honest, I don't think she's worth it. Her fiancé was killed in Iraq, he was in the same unit as Jay. She doesn't really talk about it much, but that's the only reason Henry hired her."

I nodded. "Okay, who else?"

"Deanna Spence. She's our dog trainer. She isn't ex-military, but her husband is. They own a security dog training company, and she works with us as a volunteer. Sweet lady, and I know she doesn't do the things the letter said."

We chatted a bit more, but I wasn't getting anything out of it, so I left a few minutes later. I didn't know what else to do at the moment, so I went to check on Jay. I found Gwen there with him, and Sylvi walked in just after I did. She'd gone to their house to get Gwen a change of clothes and her makeup.

"Well," I said, "I wish I had better news, but so far I'm not coming up with anything earth shattering. I went by SAVE and talked to Leigh—she's been made acting director, and by the way, she says there's no way she'd ever believe you're guilty."

Jay nodded slowly. "Leigh's a good woman. She loved Henry."

"I talked with her about the others who got the letters. One thing that struck me was that she said the doctor is gay; Sylvi made a good point that this whole thing smells like a woman's handiwork. I'm wondering if that might include a gay doctor?"

"Doc Morgan? Nah, he ain't like that, no way. He's one of the nicest people you'd ever want to meet, and he don't even act gay, you know what I mean? If I didn't know it from working with Henry, I'd never have guessed. It ain't him."

"Okay. What about the secretary? What can you tell me about her?"

Jay looked lost. "Zandra? I don't know her at all, not really. She's there a lot, but I don't really talk to her."

"Okay, I'd have thought you would. She said her fiancé was in your unit, and was killed in Iraq."

"Fiance? When was this?"

I shrugged. "Must have been over a year ago, she's been there that long. According to Leigh, the only reason she got the job was because her fiancé was supposed to have been close to you."

Jay closed his eyes in concentration. "There was a guy about a year, year and two months ago, was killed by accident; friendly fire. I wasn't there, but I knew him. Bairre Devlin, that was his name, but he wasn't never engaged. He had some woman that was stalkin' him, as I recall, and didn't want nothin' to do with women 'til he got out, he said."

Sylvi looked at me, and motioned with her head for us to leave. I told Jay and his wife I'd be back in touch, and we walked out.

On the way to the parking lot, Sylvi asked, "Are we thinking the same thing?"

I nodded. "Yeah. We need to talk to the secretary, but I need you to do some digging for me, first." I told her what I had in mind, and she got into her car to head for the office and her computer.

I went to see Mick, and ran over what I was planning with him. The case was outside his jurisdiction, because the SAVE office was actually in a suburb, not in the city itself, so he couldn't help much, but he said it sounded like my logic was pretty sound. By the time I left, I was fairly sure I was on the right track.

I got back to the office and Sylvi showed me what she'd managed to find.

Five

It was almost four PM when I was ready to put it all into play. I had Sylvi call Zandra, the secretary, and tell her we needed her help to clear up some anomalous information in SAVE's records, and that she might be helpful in proving that Leigh was fiddling the books. She said she'd be only too glad to help, and would be right over. When she got there, I apologized and said I'd be tied up for a bit, and asked Sylvi to keep her company while I finished up some paperwork.

Zandra was not an extremely pretty woman, but she wasn't ugly, either. Sylvi asked her where she'd gotten the dress she was wearing, and the two of them started chatting like old girlfriends.

"It just looks stunning on you!" Sylvi said, buttering her up. "I'm too darn skinny for a dress like that, y'know? Not enough junk in this trunk, but that makes your butt look awesome." She sighed. "You don't know what I'd give to have a body like yours!"

"Oh, girl," Zandra said, "you best be careful what you wish for! You get this kinda bump goin' on, you ain't got nothing but men all over you, all hours of the day and night! It may look like a blessing, but it's a curse, baby, it's a curse!"

"You know, I can see that," Sylvi said, and I thought she deserved an Oscar. "Is that how you met your fiancé? What was his name?"

"Bairre. He was just the most wonderful man! I thought I was gonna die when he got killed, but you know,

51

he saved his entire unit that day! He was the only one who stood up and started shooting back at the snipers, and everyone else got to get away because of him. He was a real hero, and I miss him every single day!"

"That's so sad, but you must be so proud of him, too. When were you supposed to be married?"

"Oh, that's the saddest part. He was supposed to come home only two days later, on leave, and we had this big wedding all planned out. Over a hundred people were gonna be there. It was so beautiful, and the cake was over six feet tall! I had this wedding dress all made special for me, his daddy paid for it, it cost over three thousand dollars!"

I stood up and said I had to go to the bathroom, then slipped through the door into my room. A moment later I came back out, and Zandra froze when she saw the elderly couple who followed me into the office.

"Zandra," I said, "you know Mr. and Mrs. Devlin, right? Your almost in-laws?"

Mr. Devlin took one look at Zandra and turned gray with anger. "You are the most vicious liar, woman!" he said vehemently. "Our boy hated you for the things you did to him!"

His wife walked past him and got right in Zandra's face. "Our son was never engaged to you! He dated you one time, and you wouldn't leave him alone after that! He got a restraining order to keep you away from him! How could you say these things?"

I broke up the reunion. "Folks, are you sure your son never had a real relationship with this woman? That's a pretty serious accusation."

Mrs. D turned to me. "He couldn't stand her! When he left to go on his tour of duty, we started getting these threatening letters, all typed out, and they called us all sorts of filthy things! We always thought it was her, but we couldn't prove it. Then, when Bairre got killed—and it wasn't by saving his unit, it was an accident when one of his buddy's guns went off and hit him in the head—friendly fire accident, they call that—all of a sudden the letters stopped coming." She turned back to Zandra. "But I know this much—if he was still alive, this is the last woman he'd ever want anything to do with! He wouldn't have married her if she was the last woman on earth!"

Zandra screamed, "That's a lie! He loved me, I know he did! The Army killed him, and that's what took him away from me! You people, you did everything you could to keep us apart, but he was always comin' to see me when you weren't around, 'cause he loved me!"

"You're insane!" shouted Mr. D. "Our son couldn't stand you!"

"You're the crazy ones," Zandra retorted, "he loved me! He freakin' *loved* me and he hated you because you wanted to keep us apart! He wanted to marry me, but he told me how you said I wasn't good enough! You made him join the Army, and it got him killed, and now I'm the one doing what's right! I'm gonna destroy all of those bastards who killed my Bairre!"

"Your Bairre?" shouted Mrs. D. "He was *never* your Bairre!"

Zandra screamed then, and snatched up Sylvi's letter opener from her desk, brandishing it like a weapon, lunging at Mrs. Devlin. I tried to intercept, but I wasn't close enough, and I shouted a warning.

Sylvi screamed, then, a kung fu type scream, and threw herself between the two women. For a split second I would have sworn I saw the dagger plunge into her, but it was only an illusion; Sylvi had baited Zandra, and when she tried to stab at her, Sylvi spun and snatched the blade from her hand as she kicked out with one foot and knocked the crazed woman to the floor.

I moved then, landing on top of Zandra with one knee in her chest, knocking the breath from her and keeping her down.

"Call Mick!" I yelled at Sylvi, and she snatched up the phone and dialed 911. The operator said officers would respond immediately, and then patched her through to Mick Mulcahy.

"Mick," she said. "We've got the killer here at Ned's office! Can you come and handle this?"

He said he'd be there in five minutes, and he wasn't late. He arrested Zandra for attacking Mrs. Devlin and inciting trouble, but he had to call Merkel to come into the city and make the arrest for murder.

Merkel met us all at the precinct, but he refused to arrest Zandra without more proof of her guilt. Since she lived in the city, it took Mick helping to get a search warrant for her place, but by midnight, there was still no trace of the murder weapon. Without that, Merkel said he would not dismiss against Jay, nor charge Zandra with anything. The assault on Mrs. Devlin had taken place inside the city proper, so Mick had to write up the charges on that. At least that kept her in jail for the moment.

We were no closer to proving Jay was innocent of Henry's murder, and Zandra wasn't about to confess. I was still sure it had been her, but I couldn't identify a motive. Why would she kill him, when he hadn't been anywhere near Iraq when Bairre was killed?

The rest of it was fairly easy to figure out: Zandra had been infatuated with Bairre Devlin, but he wanted nothing to do with her, so she created a world of fantasy in which they were lovers. She was undoubtedly a sick, neurotic woman, so self-deluded that she probably convinced herself that they really were going to get married one day. When Bairre was killed by friendly fire, however, she'd lost hold of the last of her sanity and decided to harass and destroy as many of the people she considered responsible as possible.

Somehow, she knew Jay had been in the same unit, and that alone was enough for her to try to make him one of those responsible for Bairre's death. Jay was involved with SAVE, so she weaseled her way in and bided her time. By the time she felt ready to strike out at him, she was connecting everyone at SAVE to Bairre's death as well, so one day she began her poison letter campaign. There were probably far more letters than we'd ever know, but since she was out of the poison pen business, those people could go on with their lives and put it behind them.

I needed to get to the bottom of it before Jay and Gwen could have any hope of normal lives, and it was driving me nuts that I wasn't able to figure it out. Could it be that Zandra had a thing for Henry, and was jealous of his relationship with Leigh? No one had ever thought so. What about her psychosis? Maybe she simply attributed some of the guilt for Bairre's death to Henry just because he was Jay's friend? Still, that didn't make me feel like I was onto something that would hold up.

Sylvi had decided to go home that night, and so I turned to my old friends Sam and Dean for inspiration. Sometimes it worked. Sometimes it didn't.

In the episode I turned on, called "Dog Dean Afternoon," the only witness to a couple of strange deaths is a dog, so Dean uses a weird Indian spell to gain the ability to speak to the dog—and ends up thinking like one. He finds himself unable to resist chasing a thrown ball or stick, and wants to chase cars so bad he can taste it! He even eyeballs a poodle lustfully for a moment, until Sam gets him to walk away.

If only I had that power, I thought to myself. *I could ask dogs to spy for me on all kinds of things, and probably be able to use my own nose to track people down. That would be so awesome.*

I drifted off to sleep just as the dog that's helping Dean tries to tell him that dogs aren't really pets, but were put here on earth for some mysterious purpose. Unfortunately, the spell wears off just as he's about find out what that purpose is, and Dean is even more frustrated than ever.

Sylvi kissed me awake, and I opened one eye to find her sitting on the couch beside where I lay. I smiled at her, and she kissed me again.

"So, what's on the agenda for today?" she asked. "Get any ideas from the boys last night?"

I started to shake my head, but suddenly the memory of the episode played through my mind, and I sat up so quickly I almost knocked her off onto the floor.

"Alfie!" I said. "I need Alfie!" I rushed through a shower and got dressed, and Sylvi handed me my morning coffee.

"What's so important about seeing the dog?" she asked as I guzzled it down.

"Just a hunch," I said, "but I think Alfie might be the key to solving this whole case. Jay always took Alfie with him to SAVE, right? That means Alfie probably knows everyone there, including Zandra."

Sylvi eyed me curiously. "And that helps us how?"

"That's the part I haven't worked out yet. Come on, let's go!"

Alfie was still at the Veterinary Hospital, so I called to say I was coming to see him. The receptionist asked if I was the man who said he'd pay the bill, and I admitted it, so she told me I could pick him up if I brought a check. I snatched one from my desk and told Sylvi to make it out.

We took my car, and I got us there in record time, barely managing not to get a ticket because the cop who saw me speeding couldn't get turned around in time to chase me down. I was parking when my phone went off. It was Mick.

"Hey, Mick," I said, "what's up?"

"What's up is I just got a call from the chief of police, telling me to 'tell that psycho private dick to slow his damn car down,' so I'm delivering the message. What are you doing out on Montrose at eighty miles an hour?"

"Going to interview a potential witness. Can't talk now, I'll call you later!" I hung up and jumped out, almost forgetting to open Sylvi's door. Before I could turn around and get to it, she had it open and was climbing out.

"Never mind me," she said, "I wanna see what you're about to do! Go, I'm right behind you!"

I got inside, found the cashier and had Sylvi pay the bill. It wasn't as bad as I'd expected, only six hundred dollars, and I figured that if this worked, it would be worth every penny. They took us back to where the animals were kept, and Alfie, still bandaged but fully operational, looked up at me with a curious expression on his face.

"Hey, boy," I said. "Wanna help Ned nail a killer?"

The dog *woofed*, and Sylvi gave me a look that said she was amazed. I grinned and hooked the leash they gave me to Alfie's collar. "Come on, boy, we got work to do!"

We led him out to the car and he hopped through the window into the shotgun seat. Sylvi gave him a look, and said, "Oh, no, hot shot, girlfriend gets the good seat. You get to ride in the back!" Alfie made a low growl, but went between the buckets to get into the back, and it was my turn to look at Sylvi in awe.

"It's a gift," she said, and got in, so I stopped worrying about it and got behind the wheel. I fired the big 428 up and wheeled out of the lot, headed for SAVE's offices.

When we got there, I saw that there were only two cars in the lot, and all three of us went in together. Leigh was there with Deanna, in the front reception area, and they both brightened when they saw me leading Alfie. He trotted right up to them, and both women gave him attention for a moment before looking at me.

"Mr. Fain?" Leigh said inquisitively. "What can we do for you?"

"Alfie's been here a lot, right? And he likes everyone?" Both women nodded, looking at me as if I'd lost my mind. Leigh said, "Alfie loves everybody here. He used to run to get to Henry…"

"I'm thinking he might notice something we've all missed. Okay if I let him run loose a bit?"

She looked confused, but nodded. "Sure."

I unhooked Alfie's leash and knelt down beside him. "Okay, boy, here's the deal: Somebody came in here and killed your pal Henry. We need to know what happened. Something here might tell us, and we need you to find it! Go find it, boy!"

Alfie looked at me the same way the women had, but after a second, he got up and started walking slowly toward the office door. He paused at the entrance, and sniffed around in the air for a moment, then turned his head and looked at me. I took a step toward him, and he went on inside.

I got to the doorway in time to see him sniffing around where Henry's chair had been, and it was obvious he was a little confused. I had counted on him expecting to see his old buddy, and when it was clear that Henry wasn't there and even his chair was gone, I thought I might get a reaction that could help me form some kind of idea. I didn't know what it would be, but I was grasping at straws.

Alfie sniffed the floor under where the chair had been, and then he whined. I would bet that a dog who'd been in combat would know that a lot of blood meant someone was dead, and he could almost certainly tell that it was Henry's blood he was smelling. It had been cleaned up, but there is no way to get it all; his keen nose would find it.

He looked at me again, and then stood up to put his front paws on the desk. He sniffed all over it, and something on the right side of the desktop was getting his attention, I could tell. Just behind me, Sylvi whispered, "Look at that!"

Alfie moved to the side of the desk and sniffed that spot again, and then a low growl came from down deep in his chest. He dropped back to the floor and started smelling the carpet, then began following a scent. He walked back my way, and I moved so he could get through unimpeded, then followed again as he walked out to the reception desk. Once again he got up and sniffed the top, and again one particular spot caught his attention, almost dead center. He dropped back to all fours, and began tracking again, and this time he went down a hallway to where the dogs were kenneled during their training. I had to help by opening the door, but

60

he didn't hesitate when I did. He went through, still tracking something on the floor.

He paused at one point, and I thought he was lost, but he cast about for a moment and picked up the scent he was looking for once again. He went back to following a trail only he could detect, and the women and I went back to following him as quietly as we could. He came to a back door. I fumbled with its deadbolt for a moment before I got it open, and Alfie let me know with a growl that I was taking too long. Once it was open, he went through and into the alleyway behind the building.

He stopped again, and sniffed about for a moment before choosing a direction and heading east. He was staying close to the wall on the right and moving a bit faster, out there in the open, so we had to hurry to keep up. By the time he'd gone half a block, my mangled foot was complaining, but I told it to shut up and I'd soak it later. Alfie didn't wait for us, so we hustled to keep close to him.

Another block, and he was getting anxious, I could tell. He was growling, and it was obvious he was onto something that he thought was important. When he stopped at a dumpster, I thought he was done, but he only sniffed at it and then went on past.

Suddenly, I had a hunch what he was after, and I silently thanked Sam and Dean for the idea that would prove Jay innocent. As far as I knew, there was only one thing that he could be tracking, and if I was right, we were about to bust this case wide open.

He continued almost another block, and then veered away from the wall and crossed the alley, still sniffing. When he came to the opposite side, he looked up at several big electric boxes, the kind with industrial sized electric meters in them, and began sniffing at them one by one.

He sat down and looked at the one in the middle, and barked once, then looked at me as if to say, "Okay, dumb human, I did my part! You're the one with opposable thumbs!"

I went to the boxes, looked at the one he was indicating, and saw that the little metal seal that the power company puts on them had been broken. Someone had twisted it off, then tried to put it back and bend it so it wouldn't be noticeable, but looking closely, I saw it. I got out a handkerchief to wrap around my fingers, pulled the broken seal off and moved the little latch that held the box's cover closed, then lifted it up and out of the way.

There, in the bottom of the box, right next to probably a gillion volts of electric wiring and relays, lay a forty caliber Glock.

Sylvie got out her phone and took several pictures of it where it lay, while I got down on my knee and told Alfie what a good dog he was. I called Merkel and told him I had his murder weapon, and that I wanted it fingerprinted as soon as possible. He acted as if he didn't believe me, but agreed to come out.

Just to be safe, I called Mick, too. He agreed to ring the county crime lab and call in a favor to get someone out to us immediately. I didn't trust Merkel to do his job, but Mick said he'd get me people I could count on, and I trusted him.

Thirty minutes later, I watched as County CSI carefully spread powder over everything, including the inside of the box and its cover and seal. The prints their super digital cameras got were clean, and some of them appeared to be the same on both the cover and the gun, according to the techs.

Merkel had arrived after the CSI team, and stood there fuming because they wouldn't let him touch anything until they were done. By the time he got the gun, it was bagged and tagged, and all he could do was escort it to the lab for ballistics testing.

Six

Mick kept track for me of the lab's work, and called me that afternoon to tell me that the prints were definitely Zandra's, and the gun was definitely the one used to kill Henry Ochoa. A trace of its serial number revealed that it had been reported stolen almost three years before, and the previous owner was a former beau of Zandra Daymude. He had been a security guard. Like Bairre, he had dated her only a couple of times, but then she acted as though he belonged to her, so he cut her off and got a restraining order to stop her stalking him. The gun was stolen about a week after that, out of his car. Odds on, she had actually planned to use it on him, but either chickened out or just never got the chance.

With all of that evidence, Merkel graciously asked the prosecutor's office to dismiss the charges against Jay, and file new ones against Zandra. Under direct interrogation, and with only a public defender to protect her rights (that's a joke, folks), she caved in and confessed to killing Henry.

He'd been bored that evening after Jay left, and had gone out to the reception area to grab a magazine, digging through the stacks for one he hadn't read a hundred times before. Zandra hadn't actually left yet, but had only gone out to put some things into her car. When she came back inside, she heard him say, "What the hell..." as he flipped through a magazine that had words and letters cut out of many of its pages. He knew instantly that the poison pen letters had been made right here in the office, and when he looked up and saw Zandra standing in his doorway looking guilty, he knew who'd done it.

She had her big purse slung over her shoulder, and when he started to shout at her and demand to know why she'd done it, she shoved a hand down into it and pulled out the Glock. She'd fired without even realizing she'd pulled the trigger, and then panicked. She had thought about trying to clean up and get rid of the body, but then it hit her that Jay had been the last one to come in. She decided to frame him for the murder, use it to destroy him over what had happened to Bairre. The only problem was that there was no way to plant the gun on him, so she wanted to get rid of it.

Knowing the scene of the crime would be searched, she'd gone out the back door looking for a hiding place, and walked down the alley to get farther from the office. When she couldn't find anything easily that wouldn't be an obvious hiding spot, she kept going, and the saw the big power boxes. She used a key to twist off the seal, put the gun inside and closed it back up. If it weren't for Alfie, the power company said, it might have been years before anyone had reason to inspect that seal or open that box. Case closed, and I was pretty darn proud of myself.

That evening, Sylvi and I were invited to Jay and Gwen's home to help them celebrate, and we were happy to go. Sylvi looked over at me as we rode in my car to their house, and said, "You know, this is the first time we've been invited to visit friends as a couple."

I smiled. "Yeah," I said. "Hopefully it won't be the last, though."

We were sitting on their back deck, enjoying iced tea and lemonade, while Jay was grilling steaks. Gwen had just told us that Alfie was doing very well, and the bandages could probably come off in a couple more days, when the doorbell rang.

Gwen and Sylvi went to answer it, and came back a moment later with Mick Mulcahy.

"Hey, everyone, I'm not here to interrupt," he said, "but I just got word that the newspaper has heard all about how Alfie tracked down the murder weapon, and they're doing a story on him for the weekend edition. The mayor, who is never one to miss a photo opportunity or a chance to get some good press, called my chief and said he wants to present Alfie with a medal. They're planning a big ceremony tomorrow afternoon, in the mayor's office at city hall; can you bring him and make it?"

Jay stood there frozen for a long moment, and then tears began to flow. He smiled at Mick, and said, "Oh, we'll be there, Mr. Mulcahy, we'll be there! Thank you, sir, thank you!"

Gwen touched Mick's arm. "Mr. Mulcahy, won't you join us? We've got plenty of steaks, and they've only just gone on the grill; it's no trouble to add another."

Mick started to beg off, but Sylvi put a stop to it.

"Don't even think about it, Mick! You're part of this celebration, too, y'know! You deserve to be here."

"Me? This wasn't even my case! I didn't have anything to do with it!"

"Yeah, you did," I growled at him. "Remember when I called you about Alfie, and you had to stop the animal cops from putting him down? Wasn't for that, he'd have been dead, and we'd still have Jay in jail for a murder he didn't commit, so sit your ass down and grab a glass!"

He stood there for a second, then grinned. "I will," he said, "on one condition. I want to know how Alfie knew what you wanted him to do. You tell me that, and I'll stay."

Everyone else, including Sylvi, demanded I answer him, so I looked at Alfie and said, "How about it, boy? Can I give away our secret?" Alfie barked, and we all laughed.

"Okay, here it is," I began. "I didn't know what I was hoping to find when I went to get Alfie, but I figured if he was familiar with the SAVE offices and knew everyone there, he might just spot something wrong if I took him back. I didn't have any expectations, exactly, just a gut hunch. When he went into Henry's office, he could tell from the smell of Henry's blood that his old buddy was dead, I think, and I guess he wanted to know why. He sniffed around the office, and sparked up on part of the desk, right about in front of where the shot would have been fired from. To me, that means he picked up the scent of the gun. Once he had that, he could follow it out of Henry's office to the front desk, where Zandra probably stopped and put the gun down to try to think through what to do. He found the scent again on that desk; then she must have picked it up again and carried it through the building, out the back, and down the alley to where she hid it."

Mick shook his head. "You're saying Alfie tracked the smell of the metal gun all that way? Come on, Ned."

I shook my head. "Hear me out. He followed the smell, not of the gun itself, but of the burnt gunpowder. Any ballistics tech knows that once you fire a gun, there is powder residue on every part of it, and on the person who fired it. Well, that powder falls off, as we move around, or as air moves over the gun, whatever, in little specks we humans would never be able to detect. But Alfie, there, being a breed of dog that is used for tracking in some countries, could smell those tiny little specks and track them where they dropped off of Zandra and the gun. She left a trail of breadcrumbs, and Alfie was the only one who could possibly have followed them."

Everyone shook their heads, and I smiled. Alfie looked around and barked a couple of times, so I'm pretty sure he knew everyone thought he was a truly wonderful dog.

We all sat quietly for a moment, and then Sylvi reached over and took my big, ugly hand in her tiny, beautiful one. I raised my glass into the air. "To those," I said solemnly, "who have fought; to those who have fallen; to those who continue to fight!"

All of us clinked glasses, and Alfie looked up at us and barked once. I looked at the dog for a moment, and then added, "And to Henry, who strove for all of us."

We clinked once more, and then we all felt a chill run down our spines, as Alfie raised his nose to the sky and howled. It was a time for mourning, and for just a moment, we all joined in with the dog and mourned his friend who was with us no more.

The end.

If you enjoyed this story, please leave a review. Your words really mean a lot.

Get a FREE *unpublished* Ned Fain story and be among the first to hear about Sam's new book releases and special deals when you join his email list here:

http://www.mix-booksonline.com/sam-abbott-insiders

Get more adventures with tough, sometimes cynical private eye, Ned Fain for one low price:

Ned Fain Private Investigator Series: Books 1 - 6

And see all of Ned's books here:
http://www.mix-booksonline.com/category/sam-abbott

Sam Abbott

...is a pseudonym for a popular author of adventure and cozy mystery. Who is that, you ask? Well, that's another mystery.

Join Sam on his facebook page:
https://www.facebook.com/SamAbbottAuthor

If you enjoyed this book, you might also like these:

- Adventure/Mystery – **The Captain Finn Treasure Mysteries:**
    o The Mystery of the One-Armed Man
    o Black Bart is Dead
    o The Gold Doubloon Mystery
    o The Game's a Foot
- Adventure/Mystery – **The Agency Confidential series:**
    o Deceit
    o Cheat